Where Is Blackbeard's Ship?

By Patricia West

Strategy Focus

As you read, **monitor** your understanding of what happened to a famous pirate ship. Reread to **clarify** your understanding of the key vocabulary.

HOUGHTON MIFFLIN   BOSTON

Key Vocabulary

plaques flat signs with words carved on them

shipwreck a wrecked or ruined ship

survivors people who face danger but are still alive

unsinkable impossible to sink

voyage a long journey

wreckage what is left of something that has been destroyed

Word Teaser

These people usually feel very lucky. Who are they?

About 300 years ago, a pirate named Blackbeard was the captain of a ship called the *Queen Anne's Revenge*. For years, Blackbeard robbed other ships that sailed along the coast of the Atlantic Ocean.

Blackbeard used his stolen money to build a castle on St. Thomas Island in the Caribbean Sea. He built a tower near the castle to watch for enemies.

Blackbeard's Tower

People thought that Blackbeard's ship seemed unsinkable. But then, on a voyage in the year 1718, it finally went down. It sank off the coast of North Carolina, in the Atlantic Ocean. Blackbeard escaped alive.

A ship from Blackbeard's time

The Discovery

No one knew exactly where Blackbeard's ship sank. Then, in 1996, explorers found parts of a sailing ship off the coast of North Carolina. This shipwreck was probably Blackbeard's ship.

The explorers found many things in the ship's wreckage. One interesting discovery was a bronze bell that had the date 1709 on it. The explorers knew that Blackbeard's ship sank just nine years after that date.

Divers found a heavy cannon buried in the sand. They also saw other cannons, and two large anchors.

A cannon from the ship's wreckage

Some people thought the *Queen Anne's Revenge* would be full of stolen gold. But explorers found only a tiny bit of gold in the shipwreck. The gold weighed less than a single penny!

The ship's survivors probably grabbed most of the gold before the ship sank. They may have escaped from the wreck in another boat.

Coins from another shipwreck about 300 years ago

Today you can see many objects that the divers found. They are in a museum in North Carolina.

Someday, divers might find old plaques carved with the name *Queen Anne's Revenge*. Then they finally will be sure they discovered Blackbeard's ship!

A brass plaque on the steering wheel of a ship today

Putting Words to Work

1. If you didn't know the meaning of the word **plaques**, on page 12, how could you figure it out?

2. How might **survivors** escape from a sinking ship?

3. Would you enjoy diving to look at **shipwrecks**? Why or why not?

4. Look at the headings in the book. Where would you find out about Blackbeard's **voyage**? Where would you find information about the **wreckage**?

5. **PARTNER ACTIVITY:** Think of a word you learned in the book. Explain its meaning to your partner and give an example.

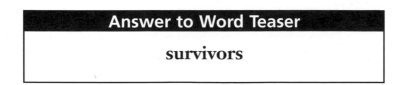

Answer to Word Teaser
survivors